Dear Rebecca, Winter Is Here

by Jean Craighead George

pictures by Loretta Krupinski

HarperCollins*Publishers*

JAc
Geo

The illustrations in this book were painted with Gouache opaque
watercolor with colored pencil.

Dear Rebecca, Winter Is Here
Text copyright © 1993 by Jean Craighead George
Illustrations copyright © 1993 by Loretta Krupinski
Printed in the U.S.A. All rights reserved.

Library of Congress Cataloging-in-Publication Data
George, Jean Craighead, date
   Dear Rebecca, winter is here / by Jean Craighead George ; pictures
by Loretta Krupinski.
       p.   cm.
   Summary: A grandmother explains to her granddaughter how the
arrival of winter brings changes in nature and the earth's creatures.
   ISBN 0-06-021139-3. — ISBN 0-06-021140-7 (lib. bdg.)
   [1. Winter—Fiction.   2. Seasons—Fiction.   3. Nature—Fiction.
4. Grandmothers—Fiction.]   I. Krupinski, Loretta, ill.   II. Title.
PZ7.G2933De   1993   92-9515
[E]—dc20   CIP
                                                                       AC

Typography by Christine Kettner
1   2   3   4   5   6   7   8   9   10
❖
First Edition

Author's Note

The Earth revolves around the sun spinning on its axis, which is tilted 23.5 degrees away from the perpendicular. When its north pole is inclined as far toward the sun as it can be, the summer solstice occurs in the northern hemisphere. This happens about June 21, and it is the longest day of the year. After June 21, the days get shorter until the north pole is tilted away from the sun, about December 21. This is the winter solstice.

Day and night are of equal length at the spring and autumn equinoxes. These occur around March 21 and September 21.

The solstices mark the big changes in the light, and life on Earth responds to these changes. In December, plants and animals get ready to breed or flower because of the lengthening minutes of daylight. In June, the light decreases, and plants and animals prepare for rest and dormancy.

—J.C.G.

MARCH 21

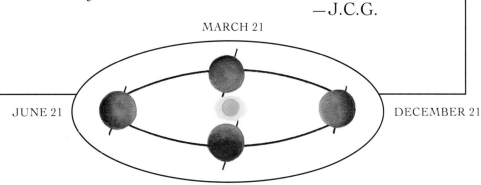

JUNE 21

DECEMBER 21

SEPTEMBER 21

Dear Rebecca,

I turned on the lights to eat breakfast this morning and put on my coat to go outside.

Winter is here.

It was brought by little hands of darkness. Each little hand is a few minutes long.

In summer they began bringing winter. They pulled the night over the edges of the dawn and dusk and made the days shorter. On June 21, while you were cooling off under the hose, winter began.

The little hands cut off the warm sunlight.

And the northern half of the Earth grew cold.

The cold ground cooled
the air until you and I
breathed tiny crystals of ice.
"Winter is here," we say.
It is here, but you can't
touch it or serve it snacks.
You can't read it a book
or make it do anything.
But it makes us do all
sorts of things.

I turn on my lights.
You put on your mittens.
The birds fly to the
sunny underside of the
Earth.

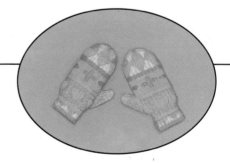

The streams stop flowing
and turn to ice.
The rain clouds of
summer become the snow
clouds of winter.

The groundhogs and
bears go to sleep.

The frogs and turtles cuddle down in the mud below the frost line.

The squirrels insulate their homes with dry leaves.

The flowers die and form winter-proof seeds.
    With the flowers gone, the bees stay home and eat honey.

The wolves leave their
cramped nursery dens and
run free on the wild ridges.

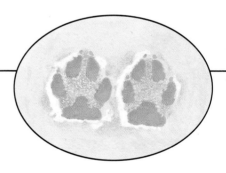

Otters make slides in
the snow.
Mice make snow tracks.

Snow birds leave the blizzard-bound mountains and come to your yard. They make tiny angel wings when they fly.

You flop and make angel wings.

I light the fire in my fireplace.

You sing jolly songs with your friends.

And while you are singing, summer begins.

On the 22nd of December, little hands of light begin to push back the edges of darkness minute by minute.

Before very long, you
will take off your shoes and
jump over bluebells.
I will eat my breakfast
outdoors in the sunshine.

The birds will return as the days grow longer. The frogs and turtles will come out of the warm mud, and the next thing you know, I'll be writing:

Dear Rebecca, summer is here.

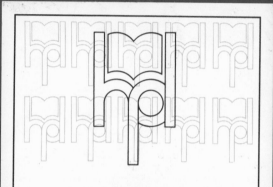